This edition published by Parragon in 2013
Parragon
Chartist House
15–17 Trim Street
Bath BA1 1HA, UK
www.parragon.com

ISBN 978-1-4723-1079-8

Printed in China

Rapunzel

Retold by Anne Marie Ryan

Illustrated by Natalie Hinrichsen

Bath • New York • Singapore • Hong Kong • Cologne • Delhi
Melbourne • Amsterdam • Johannesburg • Shenzhen

Once upon a time, a man and his wife lived in a little cottage in the shadow of a tall tower. They were very poor, but very happy.

On the other side of their garden wall was a vegetable patch. It was full of tasty-looking carrots, cabbages, and tomatoes. But there was never anyone in the patch.

"Why should all those vegetables go to waste when we're hungry?" the man asked his wife.

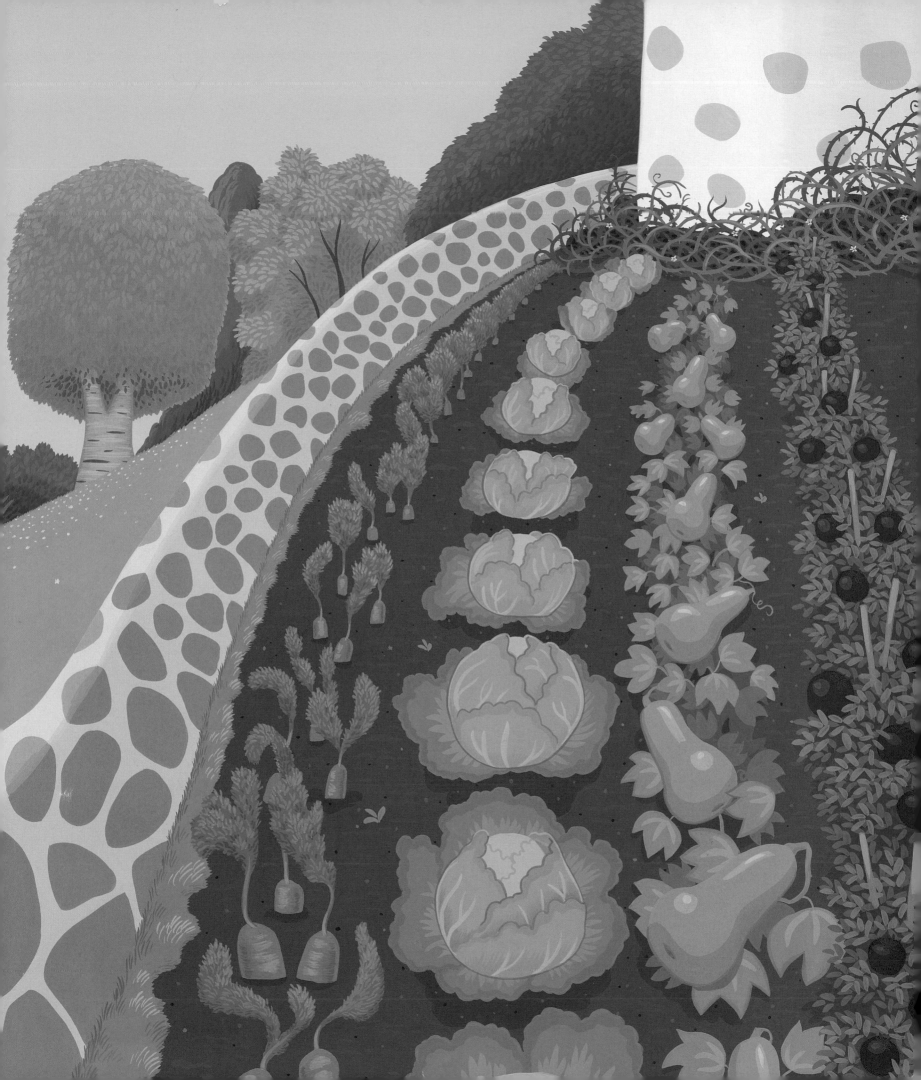

So he climbed over the wall and quickly filled his basket. As he pulled a carrot out of the ground, he heard an angry voice.

"Who said you could take MY vegetables?"

It was the old witch who owned the tower! She threatened to cast an evil spell on the man and his wife.

"Please don't hurt us," begged the man. "My wife is going to have a baby!"

"I will let you go," said the witch, "but you must give me the baby when it is born. I will care for it and treat it as my own."

The man was so scared he agreed to everything the witch asked.

Soon the man's wife had a baby girl, and the very next day the witch took the baby away.

The witch named the baby **Rapunzel**.

The baby grew into a beautiful girl.

But when Rapunzel was twelve years old, the witch locked her in a room at the top of the tower, afraid that someone might take her away.

A year or two passed and Rapunzel grew taller and her hair grew longer.

Poor Rapunzel was lonely and wished she had a friend. She would gaze out of the window, looking at the beautiful forest outside, brushing her golden hair, and singing sad, sweet songs to herself.

"How I wish the witch would set me free.
There's a great big world I long to see."

One day, a prince was riding in the forest near the tower. He heard Rapunzel singing and was enchanted by her voice.

The prince hid behind a bush and listened.

Soon, the witch arrived at the bottom of the tower and called out,

"Rapunzel, Rapunzel, let down your hair."

Beautiful Rapunzel appeared at the window and let down her long, golden hair for the witch to climb up.

The next day, the prince watched the witch slide down Rapunzel's hair.
When he was sure that the witch was far away, the prince called out,

"Rapunzel, Rapunzel, let down your hair."

Down tumbled the long,
golden hair and up climbed
the prince.

At first, Rapunzel was frightened of the stranger. But they quickly became friends.

Rapunzel loved hearing the prince's stories.

He told her how it felt to run barefoot in a grassy meadow ...

and how it felt to swim in the cold, blue sea. Rapunzel had never done such things.

"I will help you escape from the tower," promised the prince.

The next day, and for many days after, the prince visited Rapunzel whenever the witch went out.

Every time, he would call out,

"Rapunzel, Rapunzel, let down your hair."

And every time, he brought silk string for Rapunzel to weave into a ladder so she could, one day, climb down the tower and escape.

Rapunzel worked on the ladder in secret and soon it nearly reached the ground.

The witch knew nothing of this until once, without thinking, Rapunzel said, "Oh, you are so much heavier than the prince when you climb!"

The witch was very angry.

She grabbed the scissors from Rapunzel's sewing basket and cut up the ladder.

SNIP! SNIP! SNIP!

Then the witch cut off Rapunzel's long, golden hair and cast a spell, banishing Rapunzel deep into the forest.

Still angry, the witch waited until she heard the prince call out,

"Rapunzel, Rapunzel, let down your hair."

Down to the ground tumbled Rapunzel's long, golden hair and up climbed the prince.

"Ha!" cried the witch, when the prince reached the top. "You've come for Rapunzel, but she has gone, and you'll never find her!"

Shocked, the prince

f
e
l
l

from the tower, into a thorn bush on the ground. The bush broke his fall, but the thorns scratched his eyes, making him blind.

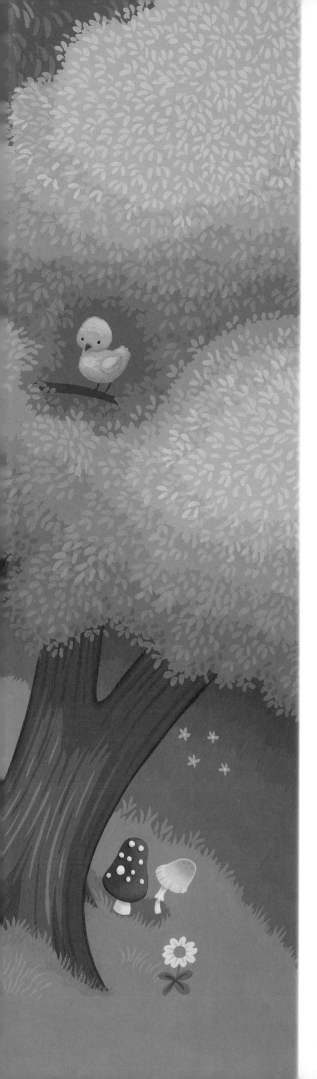

For many months, the blind prince wandered through the wilderness. Everywhere he went, he called, "Rapunzel! Rapunzel! Where are you?"

One day, he heard a sad, sweet song float through the woods.

"As I roam from tree to tree,
My true love's face I long to see."

"Rapunzel! Rapunzel!" he called, "Is that you?"

Rapunzel ran through
the woods and hugged the prince.

"I've found you at last!" she cried.

Rapunzel's tears of joy fell into the prince's eyes
and he could see once more! Rapunzel's long hair was short now,
but she was still as beautiful as ever.

Rapunzel and the prince never saw the witch again and they
traveled the world together, visiting all the wonderful sights
Rapunzel had longed to see. And they lived happily ever after!

The End